THE GLOBETROTTERS
GO TO
FRANCE

This book has been designed to give
children a fun introduction to the geography
of France and an entertaining
insight into the French way of life.

The story and pictures in this book
are all original and have been specially
commissioned for Tesco.

Published for Tesco Stores Limited
Created by Brilliant Books Ltd
84–86 Regent Street
London W1R 5PA

First published 2000

Text and illustrations © 2000 Brilliant Books Ltd
Printed by Printer Trento S.r.l., Italy
Reproduction by Colourpath, England

fun to learn

collection

THE GLOBETROTTERS
GO TO
FRANCE

Written by **Rachel Warren Chadd**
Illustrated by **Stephen May**

It was chaos as usual in the Trotter household as Rosie and
Harry rushed into the hallway to get the post. Rosie grabbed
an envelope with a French stamp on it, addressed to 'M. Trotter'.

"What does 'M' stand for? No one's name begins with 'M'.
Unless it's for Mum," she said.

"No, Rosie. It means 'Monsieur' – French for 'Mr'," said Dad,
putting on his glasses and opening the letter. "Aunt Émilie
is inviting us to visit her and old Uncle Félix for
his 80th birthday," he said.

"Ooh," said Mum. "At their château? How very exciting!"

They all looked at their map to see where they would be going. But Dad looked worried. "She says Uncle Félix is not at all well. He always had such a good appetite – but now he won't eat anything."

"I'm not surprised," Harry whispered to Rosie. "French food is disgusting! But we don't need to worry – I've got a plan. Listen..."

Paris

FRANCE

Mt. Blanc
Lyons

Grasse

The family had to leave from Waterloo Station in London.

"Next stop, PARIS," said Dad settling into his seat. "It's 200 miles away, but we'll be there in three hours. We'll be travelling at up to 180mph when we get on the French stretch of track!"

Harry and Rosie munched flaky French croissants from the buffet (which weren't disgusting at all!).

"Eurostar's brilliant," said Harry, as they arrived in Paris. "I wasn't even scared when we went through the Channel Tunnel under the sea!"

Dad's cousin Michel met them at GARE DU NORD STATION.
He told them all about poor old Uncle Félix.

"We 'ave been so worried about 'im. We must create for 'im
a great birthday feast, and get 'im eating like a real pig again!"
he said. Michel was a famous French chef and was very passionate
about food. "Ze English food eez how you say… 'disgusting'.
Per'aps you can find 'im something to eat 'ere. I shall take 'im
some delicious 'escargots' - that's snails!" smiled Michel.

Harry nudged Rosie and mouthed, "Yukky, yuk!"

Yukky, yuk!

Paris was great fun. First they went to the EIFFEL TOWER:
"Height - 300 metres. Weight - 7,000 tons. Age - 111 years,"
said Dad, who loved facts. He even made them all count
the 1,652 steps to the top, where Harry launched
a superb paper plane and watched it fly down
towards the RIVER SEINE below.

Eiffel Tower -
height 300 metres

Next they explored the CATHEDRAL O[...]
Harry made faces at the gargoyles.

"Stop it!" hissed Mum.

"Well, they started it!" Harry [...]
started calling out: "Where's th[...]

Dad pulled Rosie away from [...]
photograph, and decided it w[...]
a relaxing evening's entertainment...

Next mor[...]
LYONS,[...]
kept[...]

...ning, when they took another really fast train to
...Dad had a very nasty headache and Rosie and Harry
...giggling as they remembered the night before.

"I got a picture," whispered Rosie. "Dad looked so silly
dancing on the table. I think he drank too much wine!"

Mum overheard. "He was just tasting it. He wanted to know
if it was good enough to take to Uncle Félix," she said crossly.

"And it's traditional to dance the cancan in Paris," groaned
Dad, holding his head. "It would have been rude not to.
Now just you behave yourselves and quieten down."

It's traditional

Dad's cousin Henri, his wife Cathérine and their children Jules and Madeleine met them at Lyons and whisked them away in a large Citroën car – out of the city and along the banks of the RIVER RHÔNE.

"I love France," said Dad, whose headache was clearing. "There's so much space. A few more people than Britain perhaps, but nearly twice as much land!"

"And we 'ave beautiful mountains," said Henri.

"See ahead, 'zat is MONT BLANC, 4,800 metres 'igh. Now we are going to drive through ze famous tunnel under ze ALPS. Zen you can say you 'ave been to Italy. After zat we will drive back to ze chalet."

The following morning they all went skiing. "'Ere we can ski, even in summer. Is zat not fantastique?" said Henri.

On the slopes, Harry was a dare-devil. "Come back, it eez too steep," shouted Jules. But Harry was zooming down the slope, faster and faster till… SPLAT!

He looked so silly, Rosie took a picture.

"This is bound to make Uncle Félix laugh," she giggled.

When they got back to the chalet, Harry was very hungry, but he was dreading what he might have to eat. Mum had been shopping and there was a strong smell of garlic and really stinky cheese. To Harry's delight, this was not for them.

"Frites for the enfants," shouted Henri, as a huge pile of crispy chips appeared.

"Dip them in mayonnaise, they're delicious," said Jules. Harry wasn't sure about having mayonnaise with chips at first, but he soon got used to the idea. He even wondered if 'frites' might tempt the appetite of poor Uncle Félix.

"Phew! We can keep my emergency supplies for another day," he whispered to Rosie, as he finished his third plateful.

That afternoon, after they had changed, the children went cycling in the foothills of the Alps. Among all the twists and turns, Harry lost sight of Jules for a while, but suddenly spotted his yellow jumper ahead and gave chase – faster and faster and faster.
Then he noticed people cheering him from the side of the road. "How strange!" he thought.

there he goes

Suddenly there was a great whooshing noise, and Harry
was swallowed up in a sea of bikes, which included Jules.

"We 'ave got caught up in ze Tour de France – it is
ze big international cycle contest!" puffed Jules.
"I zink per'aps you were following ze leader
who 'as a yellow jersey like mine."

"Oh no!" said Harry. "I thought I was following *you*!"

Mum wanted to buy some scent in the famous town of GRASSE, so the next day they all set off on a great perfume tour! In the scent factory, Rosie was entranced with the wonderful smells. There were casks of perfume with little taps, and when no one was looking she quickly turned on a tap and put her hanky under it to soak up the perfume. But she couldn't turn it off. It went everywhere!

Rosie panicked and fled.

"PWAR!" cried Harry, pinching his snout.

"I'm not getting in the car with you!"

Rosie still stank when they arrived at their next destination – the wine-making region of BORDEAUX. Here, among the beautiful vineyards laden with grapes, stood Uncle Félix's great château.

Michel had arrived from Paris for the party too. He was carrying a huge dish of snails – ready for the feast!

Michel wanted the dinner to be unforgettable, and he took them shopping to the local market to buy everything for the big night. Huge tomatoes, fat olives, pâtés, heads of garlic, fresh herbs - wherever Michel pointed, stall holders wrapped and packed. "I choose ze very best for poor Félix," he declared.

Dozens of fishy eyes stared at Harry as Michel picked out lobsters, snails and a jar of something called 'foie gras' which looked horrid but was still incredibly expensive. Harry felt ill and was just glad he'd made his own plans for supper...

Aunt Émilie and her dogs came out to greet them when they got back. "Sssh children! You must be very quiet. Félix is really very sick, I'm afraid, and 'e's sleeping."

"Don't worry," said Michel. "My cooking is irresistible!"

But when Félix came down to supper that night, and looked at the food spread out before him, he just sat there looking sad, and he didn't touch a thing.

Neither did Harry. He gave all his food to the dogs. But he wasn't worried – he knew with his secret hoard, there was no chance of him going to bed hungry.

The next day was Uncle Félix's birthday! He smiled and said "merci" for all his presents and gave Rosie a kiss, because she had been out to pick him a bunch of flowers.

"Would you like to see all the funny pictures we've taken of our trip? You must see my photo of Dad doing the cancan!" Rosie said.

"I would be enchanted!" smiled Uncle Félix.

"Yes, and you can show us some of your magic tricks - Dad has told us all about them!" said Harry.

"Don't get 'im tired," whispered Aunt Émilie sternly, as Uncle Félix went off to play with the children.

They got on so well, they spent all morning together.
Then Aunt Émilie came and asked what they wanted for lunch.

"Can we have anything?" asked Harry. "I've brought
something from home that I thought Uncle Félix might like."

"Ah, as you wish," smiled Aunt Émilie. "It won't do any good,
but you might as well try. After all, 'e won't eat anysing else!"

Harry rushed upstairs and reappeared with
a lumpy-looking bag, which he handed over
to a surprised French cook.

Shortly afterwards Mum and Dad heard whoops of laughter coming from the children's room.

"Pipe down!" shouted Dad sternly, as he rushed off to see what was going on. "Don't you realise Uncle Félix is ill! Have a little consideration, please!"

But when Dad went in, he couldn't believe his eyes. "Just look at this!" he called to Michel and Henri.

Just look at this

There was Uncle Félix, looking very sheepish,
with tomato sauce all round his mouth, stirring up
a huge plate of mashed potato and baked beans.
   "C'est magnifique!" he declared.

C'est magnifique

Beans, beans...

That night, at his birthday dinner, Uncle Félix would only eat baked beans. Michel, the great French chef, had steam coming out of his ears! He said it was an insult to French cooking. Aunt Émilie was delighted that Félix was eating again. Dad and Mum smiled — though they couldn't quite understand how Harry had managed to hide so many tins in his bag. And Rosie and Harry started teaching their French cousins a little rhyme..."Beans, beans, good for your heart. The more you eat, the more you..."